PIC
WEL

Wells, Rosemary

Mama, don't go!

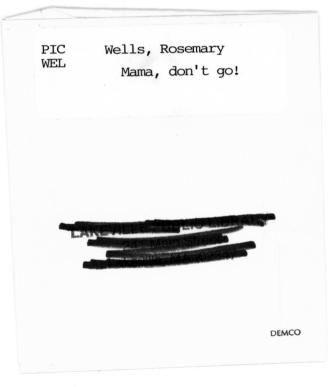

DEMCO

YOKO & FRIENDS
SCHOOL DAYS

Mama, Don't Go!

Text and jacket art by
Rosemary Wells

Interior illustrations by
Jody Wheeler

VOLO

Hyperion Books for Children
New York

Printed in the United States of America

First Edition
1 3 5 7 9 10 8 6 4 2

LIBRARY OF CONGRESS CATALOGING-IN-PUBLICATION DATA
Wells, Rosemary.
Mama, don't go! / Rosemary Wells.
p.   cm.— (Yoko and friends—school days ; 1)
Summary: Yoko loves kindergarten, but she doesn't want her mother to leave—
until her new friend helps her realize that "mothers always come back."
ISBN 0-7868-0720-2 (hardcover)—ISBN 0-7868-1526-4 (pbk.)
[1. Cats—fiction. 2. Kindergarten—Fiction. 3. Separation anxiety—Fiction.
4. Schools—Fiction.] I. Title.
PZ7.W46843 Mam 2001
[E]—dc21 00-57263

Visit www.hyperionchildrensbooks.com

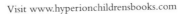

Yoko could not wait

for the first day of school.

She wanted to say hello

to lots of new friends.

She wanted to learn all the words

to all the songs.

She wanted to play

with the beautiful silver beads

in Mrs. Jenkins's classroom.

But Yoko did not want

her mother to leave.

On Monday morning, Yoko's

mother stayed for ten minutes

after school began.

But when she put on her coat,

Yoko cried loud and hard.

Everyone got upset.

Yoko's mother sat

in the back of the classroom

for the whole morning.

On Tuesday morning,

Yoko wanted to string a necklace

of colored beads.

She could not wait to write

ABCDEFG on the blackboard.

But she was still not ready

to have her mother leave.

Yoko's mother said, "Yoko, I have to go home. I have work to do."

"Oh, no," said Yoko.

"If you leave, I will cry so much, everybody will get upset again."

So Yoko's mother could not leave.

After the alphabet song,

Yoko's mother was thirsty.

"I am going to the cafeteria

for a drink of apple juice,"

said Yoko's mother.

"Yes, but come right back,"

said Yoko.

"I will come right back,"

said Yoko's mother.

Yoko waited for her mother
to come back.

In ten minutes, her mother
came back.

"Now may I leave for an hour?"
asked Yoko's mother.

"No," said Yoko. "I am not ready
for you to leave again."

On Wednesday morning, Yoko

wanted to hear story time.

She sang the "Falling Leaves" song

with her new friend, Timothy.

But Yoko was still not ready

for her mother to leave.

At snack time, Mrs. Jenkins said,

"Oh, my goodness! We are out of

celery sticks and crackers.

We can't have snack time

with nothing to eat.

Yoko, will you let me ask

your mother to go to the store?"

Yoko turned around.

"How long will it take?"

she asked.

"Maybe fifteen minutes.

Maybe twenty,"

said Yoko's mother.

Yoko watched her mother
drive away. She stayed
at the window until her mother
came back. But she did not cry.

"Why do you worry so much
about your mother, Yoko?"
asked Timothy.
"Because I don't want her
to leave me," said Yoko.

"But she will always come back,"
said Timothy.
"I still feel afraid,"
said Yoko.

"Oh, mothers always come back,"
said Timothy. "They just come back
and come back, and after a while,
you have to ask them
to stay home."

"Ask them to stay home!" said
Yoko. "I could never do that."

"I like to surprise my mother,"
said Timothy.

"Surprise her?" asked Yoko.

"I think you should give your
mother a day off," said Timothy.

"Everyone needs a day off."

On Thursday, Yoko could not wait

to feed the goldfish.

She could not wait to sing

"The Star Spangled Banner"

with Nora and Fritz.

But Yoko was not ready

for her mother to leave.

"Do we have any birthdays today?" asked Mrs. Jenkins.

Nobody raised a hand.

"Are you sure?" asked Mrs. Jenkins.

Nobody raised a hand.

Then, from the back of the classroom, Yoko's mother raised her hand.

"It's my birthday today,"

said Yoko's mother.

"Oh, well!" said Mrs. Jenkins.

"We have to do something special."

Mrs. Jenkins asked Yoko to come up

to the front of the class.

She whispered something

in Yoko's ear.

Yoko whispered back.

Mrs. Jenkins whispered back

to Yoko.

And Yoko nodded her head.

Then Yoko ran back
to her mother.

"You have to leave now, Mama,"
said Yoko. "We're going
to make a surprise for you."
So Yoko's mother had to leave.

Yoko watched her drive

the car away.

"She'll come back," said Timothy.

"They always do."

Yoko's mother came back

at the end of the day.

The class had made a cake.

They made hats with sparkles,

and everyone sang,

"Happy Birthday, Yoko's mama!"

Yoko went home with her mother.

They had their hats

and their bead necklaces

and extra pieces of birthday cake.

"That was a wonderful surprise!"

said Yoko's mother.

"Yes, it was," said Yoko,

"but the best surprise of all

is yet to come!"

"What is it?" asked Yoko's mother.

"It's a surprise!" said Yoko.

Yoko waited until the next
morning to surprise her mother.
"I still don't have my best surprise
of all," said Yoko's mother.
"Here it is!" said Yoko.

"I can't see it!" said Yoko's mother.

"That's because it is a day off!"

said Yoko.

"A day off!" said Yoko's mother.

"You may do whatever you want

today," said Yoko.

So Yoko's mother did whatever she wanted.

And at three o'clock,

Yoko watched her mother's car

come up the school driveway.

"There she is!" said Timothy.

"They always come back,"

said Yoko.

"Next week you'll have to ask her

to stay home!" said Timothy.

"Yes, I will!" said Yoko.

Dear Parents,

When our children were young we lived in a small house, but we always made a space just for books. When their dad or I would read a story out loud, the TV was always off—radio and music, too—because it intruded.

Soon this peaceful half hour of every day became like a little island vacation. Our children are lifetime readers now with an endless curiosity for the rich world waiting between the covers of good books. It cost us nothing but time well spent and a library card.

This set of easy-to-read books is about the real nitty-gritty of elementary school. There are new friends, and bullies, too. There are germs and the "Clean Hands" song, new ways of painting pictures, learning music, telling the truth, gossiping, teasing, laughing, crying, separating from Mama, scary Halloweens, and secret valentines. The stories are all drawn from the experiences my children had in school.

It's my hope that these books will transport you and your children to a setting that's familiar, yet new. And that it will prove to be a place where you can explore the exciting new world of school together.

Rosemary Wells